THREE CHEERS FOR MOUSE MATH

Albert Is NOT Scared: **An ILA/CBC Children's Choices Selec**

A Mousy Mess: **Mathical Honor Book** for PreK-K

Albert the Muffin-Maker: **Moonbeam Children's Book Awards Bronze Medalist**

Albert the Muffin-Maker: "An enjoyable, instructive story with humor, heart and a pair of adorable mice." —***Kirkus***

"The Mouse Math series is a great way to integrate math and literacy into your early childhood curriculum."
—***Teaching Children Mathematics***

"These titles present basic concepts, thinking skills, and reading skills all wrapped up in engaging stories. . . . Not only do the adorable mice introduce math, but they also share lessons about helping others . . . and thinking about the best way to solve problems. Consider these books first purchases." —***School Library Journal***

The Mousier the Merrier!: "Melmon's tender cartoons seamlessly integrate the counting lesson into the narrative."
—***Publishers Weekly***

For my own three bugs, Larry, Ashley, and Austin—L.H.

For my favorite little bugs, Claire and Ellie—D.M.

Special thanks to Meg Susi for providing the Fun Activities in the back of this book.

Library of Congress Cataloging-in-Publication Data

Names: Harkrader, Lisa, author. | Melmon, Deborah, illustrator.
Title: The twelve-bug day / by Lisa Harkrader ; illustrated by Deborah Melmon.
Other titles: 12 bug day
Description: First edition. | New York : Kane Press, an imprint of Astra Books for Young Readers, [2022] | Series: Mouse math. | Audience: Ages 5-8. | Audience: Grades K-1. | Summary: Hoping to win lunch with famous entomologist Arizona Brown, Albert looks for all twelve bugs at the insect zoo and counts down each time he finds one.
Identifiers: LCCN 2021051216 (print) | LCCN 2021051217 (ebook) | ISBN 9781635926910 (hardcover) | ISBN 9781635925401 (trade paperback) | ISBN 9781635925418 (epub)
Subjects: CYAC: Subtraction—Fiction. | Mice—Fiction.
Classification: LCC PZ7.H27645 Tw 2022 (print) | LCC PZ7.H27645 (ebook) | DDC [E]—dc23
LC record available at https://lccn.loc.gov/2021051216
LC ebook record available at https://lccn.loc.gov/2021051217

10 9 8 7 6 5 4 3 2 1

Kane Press
An imprint of Astra Books for Young Readers, a division of Astra Publishing House
astrapublishinghouse.com
Printed in China

THE TWELVE-BUG DAY

by **Lisa Harkrader** • illustrated by **Deborah Melmon**

AN IMPRINT OF ASTRA BOOKS FOR YOUNG READERS

New York

Today was the field trip to the insect zoo! Albert scrambled into line. "A whole day at Planet Bug!" he said.

"A whole day with *Arizona Brown*'s bugs," Albert's sister Wanda whispered.

"Pair up!" said Albert's teacher, Mrs. Munch.

Albert scooted next to his friend Leo. Wanda picked Lucy.

Mrs. Munch passed out a list of bugs and a Planet Bug map. "Look for each insect on the list," she said. "The first pair to find all twelve—"

"—wins lunch with Arizona Brown."

"Arizona Brown?" Albert said.

"Arizona Brown!" The other mice cheered.

Wanda's eyes grew wide. "Arizona Brown."

Wanda's new favorite book was about Arizona Brown. Arizona Brown was smart. She was daring. She traveled the world, finding bugs.

Wanda grabbed Lucy's paws. "And we could meet her!"

Albert counted the bugs on the list.
One, two, three,
four, five, six,
seven, eight, nine,
ten, eleven, twelve.

"Twelve!" Albert swallowed. "That's a lot of bugs."

"Take it bug by bug," Mrs. Munch told him.

"I don't even have twelve fingers to count on!" Albert wailed. Could he and Leo find all twelve insects?

"Oh, no!" Leo pointed at Wanda and Lucy.

They had checked a bug off their list!

Albert pulled Leo's arm. "Let's go."

Albert heard something.

Buzzzzzzz.

"A bee! We found one!" said Albert. "How many are left?"

"Twelve bugs minus one bug is eleven bugs," said Leo.

$$12 - 1 = 11$$

They heard something else.

Chirrrrrrp.

"A cricket!" said Leo. "Now we've found two bugs. Twelve minus two is ten."

"Ten bugs left!" Albert said.

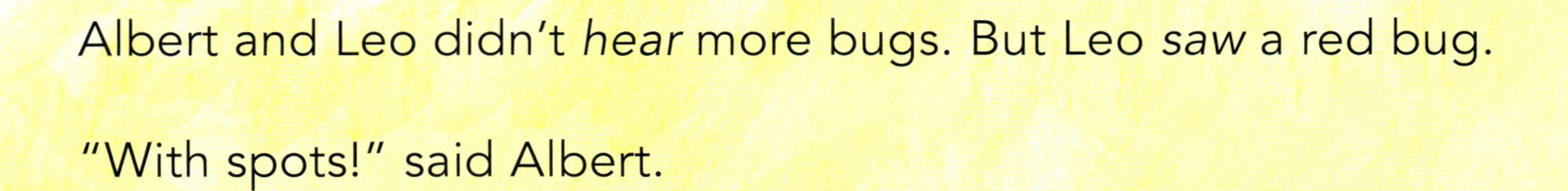

Albert and Leo didn't *hear* more bugs. But Leo *saw* a red bug.

"With spots!" said Albert.

They marked *ladybug* off the list. "Three bugs done!" said Leo.

"Twelve minus three is nine." Albert smiled. He was getting the hang of it. "Nine bugs left!"

Wanda and Lucy wandered past. Their list was covered with check marks.

Albert found a grasshopper in the desert room.
That made four bugs.
Twelve minus four was eight.

Leo found an ant.

Twelve minus five was seven.

$12 - 4 = 8$

$12 - 5 = 7$

Albert looked at their list. It was getting smaller!

But so was Wanda and Lucy's.

"Hurry!" Albert darted to the next room.

Leo found three bugs. "Twelve minus six is six," he said. "Twelve minus seven is five. Twelve minus eight is four."

$12 - 6 = 6$
$12 - 7 = 5$
$12 - 8 = 4$
$12 - 9 = 3$
$12 - 10 = 2$
$12 - 11 = 1$

Arizona Brown's
Rainforest Bugs
These insects live deep
in the hot, steamy rainforest!

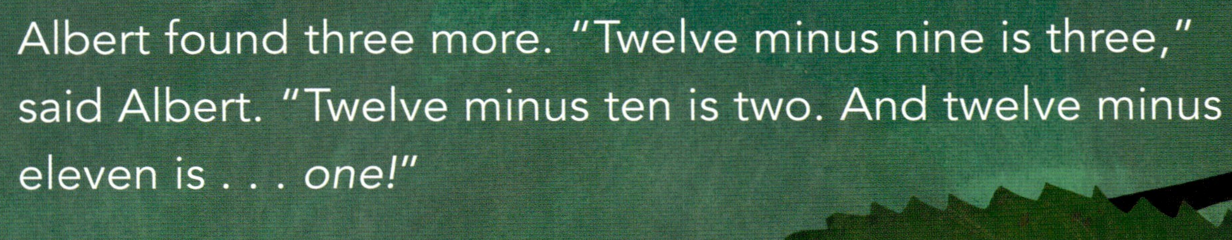

Albert found three more. "Twelve minus nine is three," said Albert. "Twelve minus ten is two. And twelve minus eleven is . . . *one!*"

Albert and Leo stared at each other. "One bug left!"

Albert checked the list. "A giant walking leaf."

Albert looked.

Leo looked.

They looked.
And looked.

They didn't see a giant walking leaf.
They only saw Wanda and Lucy.

"Hide our list," Albert whispered.

Leo stuck the list behind his back. He pressed himself against the wall. His shirt matched the wall. Leo blended in!

"Maybe a walking leaf blends in, too," Albert whispered. "With leaves!"

Albert and Leo searched the leaves.

There!

Albert pointed. Wanda pointed, too.

Twelve bugs minus twelve bugs was . . . zero bugs!

Albert and Leo and Wanda and Lucy raced to Mrs. Munch. "We found all twelve!" they cried.

"At the same time?" Mrs. Munch frowned. "We need a tiebreaker."

"Tiebreaker?" Wanda squeaked.

Wanda's face grew pale. Her paws trembled. Albert knew she really wanted to win. He pointed at Wanda's map. "They found an *extra* bug."

Wanda nodded. "A dung beetle."

"Strongest bug in the world," a voice boomed.

The mice whirled.

"Arizona Brown?" Albert said.

"Arizona Brown!" Leo and Lucy cheered.

Wanda's eyes grew wide. "Arizona Brown."

"I'd say we have a winner!" Arizona Brown put her hat on Wanda's head. She let Lucy hold her walking stick. They scurried off to eat lunch.

Leo scratched his head. "What do you get when you take two mice from a group of mice?"

"More cheese for me!" said Albert.

"I knew you could do it, Albert." Mrs. Munch smiled.

"Twelve is a lot," said Albert. "But I took it bug by bug!"

 2 # FUN ACTIVITIES  

The Twelve-Bug Day supports children's understanding of the concept of **subtracting from a two-digit number**. Use the activities below to extend the mathematics and to reinforce children's early reading skills.

ENGAGE

- Read the first two pages. Ask children if they have ever been on a field trip. Where did they go and what did they do? Invite students to predict what will happen to the mice on the field trip.
- Mrs. Munch tells the mice to *pair up*. Ask students what this means. Ask: *What comes in pairs?*
- Lead children in a picture walk through the book. Ask them what they notice and what they wonder. Invite them to make connections to what they see in the pictures. Pause after showing students the list of 12 bugs. Read the list aloud. Which types of bugs are they familiar with?

LOOK BACK

- Ask: *Why was Wanda so excited to try to find all of the bugs?*
- Draw children's attention to the subtraction equations. Ask them to use words to explain what the numbers and symbols mean.
- Ask: *Where did Leo and Albert find the walking leaf bug? Why did they look there to find it?*
- Ask: *What would you ask Arizona Brown if you had a chance to meet her? Why?*

TRY THIS!

We're Going on a Pattern Hunt!

- Make a list of 12 items that can be found in a home or classroom. Invite children to go on a scavenger hunt to find the items. As children are searching, have them pause. How many items have they found? How many items do they still need to find?
    - Ask children to explain how they figured out how many were still left.

- Children might use their fingers, draw a picture, or use objects to figure out how many they have left to find.

- Two-digit numbers are made, or **composed**, of tens and ones. For example, the number 14 is made of a group of 10 and 4 ones. When you subtract from a two-digit number, it can help to break it apart, or **decompose** it, into groups of tens and ones.
- First, draw a picture to represent the situation. Then label it with numbers and equation symbols. What do you notice about the numbers?
  - 14 mice are looking for bugs and only 3 mice have found the cricket. How many more mice need to find the cricket?
  - 14 mice are looking for bugs and 10 of the mice have found the caterpillar. How many more mice need to find the caterpillar?
  - 14 mice are looking for bugs and 13 of the mice have found the moth. How many more mice need to find the moth?
  - 14 mice are looking for bugs and 9 of the mice have found the stink bug. How many more mice need to find the stink bug?

THINK!

Pattern Superstars

- Albert uses subtraction to figure out how many more bugs he needs to find. Ask students what they know about subtraction. When in their lives would they want to know how to subtract?
- **BONUS:** Albert and Leo have found 9 out of the 12 bugs. Wanda and Lucy said they have 3 more bugs to find from the list of 12 bugs. Is it possible to predict who will finish first? Why?